This Book Belongs To:

_____

For information regarding permission write:
Books to Bed, Inc.
224 West 35th Street, Room 700, New York, NY.10001

Library of Congress Cataloging-in-Publication Data on file
ISBN 978-1-61584-794-5

First Edition - 5th Printing

Importer: Books to Bed, Inc.
Printed in China
Recommended for age 3+

Visit www.Bookstobed.com

Twas the Night before Christmas...

Illustrated By:
Alisa Grodsky
Poem By:
Clement C. Moore

Twas the night before Christmas
when all through the house
Not a creature was stirring,
not even a mouse;

The stockings were hung
by the chimney
with care,
In hopes that
St. Nicholas
soon would be there;

The children
were nestled
all snug in their beds,
While visions of
sugar-plums
danced in their heads;

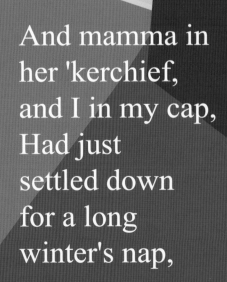

And mamma in
her 'kerchief,
and I in my cap,
Had just
settled down
for a long
winter's nap,

When out on the lawn
there arose such a clatter,
I sprang from the bed
to see what was the matter.

Away to the window
I flew like a flash,
Tore open the shutters
and threw up the sash.

The moon on the breast
of the new-fallen snow
Gave the lustre of mid-day
to objects below,

When, what to my wondering eyes should appear,
But a miniature sleigh, and eight tiny reindeer,

With a little old driver, so lively and quick,
I knew in a moment it must be St. Nick.

More rapid
than eagles
his coursers they came,
And he whistled, and
shouted, and called
them by name;

"Now, Dasher! now, Dancer!
now, Prancer and Vixen!
On, Comet! on Cupid!
on, Donder and Blitzen!

To the top of the porch!
to the top of the wall!
Now dash away! dash away!
dash away all!"

As dry leaves
that before
the wild hurricane fly,
When they meet
with an obstacle,
mount to the sky,

So up to the house-top
the coursers they flew,
With the sleigh full of toys,
and St. Nicholas too.

And then, in a twinkling,
I heard on the roof
The prancing and pawing
of each little hoof.

As I drew in my hand,
and was turning around,
Down the chimney St. Nicholas came
with a bound.

He was dressed all in fur,
from his head to his foot,
And his clothes
were all tarnished
with ashes and soot;

A bundle of toys
he had flung on his back,
And he looked like a peddler
just opening his pack.

His eyes -- how they twinkled!
His dimples how merry!
His cheeks were like roses,
his nose like a cherry!

His droll little mouth
was drawn up like a bow,
And the beard of his chin
was as white as the snow;

The stump of a pipe
he held tight in his teeth,
And the smoke
it encircled his head
like a wreath;

He had a broad face
and a little round belly,
That shook,
when he laughed
like a bowlful of jelly.

He was chubby and plump,
a right jolly old elf,
And I laughed
when I saw him,
in spite of myself;

A wink of his eye and
a twist of his head,
Soon gave me to know
I had nothing to dread;

He spoke not a word,
but went straight to his work,
And filled all the stockings;
then turned with a jerk,

And laying his finger aside of his nose,
And giving a nod, up the chimney he rose;

He sprang to his sleigh, to his team gave a whistle,
And away they all flew like the down of a thistle.

But I heard him exclaim,
ere he drove out of sight,